Nervous

Tony Norman

Illustrated by
Paul Savage

 FUL

Titles in Full Flight 3

Badger Publishing Limited
26 Wedgwood Way, Pin Green Industrial Estate,
Stevenage, Hertfordshire SG1 4QF
Telephone: 01438 356907. Fax: 01438 747015.
www.badger-publishing.co.uk
enquiries@badger-publishing.co.uk

Nervous   ISBN 1 84424 232 3

Series Editor: Jonny Zucker
Publisher: David Jamieson
Editor: Paul Martin
Design: Jain Birchenough
Cover illustration: Paul Savage

Nervous

Tony Norman

Illustrated by
Paul Savage

Contents

Badger Publishing

Chapter 1 - Dream Stars

They were all over the school.

Big colour posters that read:

Dream Stars Talent Show!

Ever dreamed of being a pop star? Here's your big chance.

The top band or singer will win:

1) A day at Red Fox Studios to make a CD single.
2) CD to be played on top local radio station Chart Zone FM.

Make your dreams come true!
Sign up now!

Lance Crane's eyes were bright with greed. As soon as he saw the sign, he knew the prize was his. He could taste the glory. His band, Elite, were so much better than the other bands at school, it was sad.

Lance sent a text to his friend, Zak, who was off school sick. He wrote:

```
GET RDY TO MAKE CD ZAK.
TALENT SHOW AT SCHOOL.
ELITE RULE, RIGHT?
```

"Looks good, doesn't it?"

Lance looked round to see who was talking. A mean smile ran across his face. The tall, tubby boy next to him was a mess. The buttons on his shirt were all in the wrong holes and his school tie was halfway round his neck.

"Hi Jools," said Lance, his voice as smooth as oil. "Yeah, great prize. Hey, how would you like to join my band for this?"

"Elite?" said Jools, amazed.

"Right. We need a keyboard player. You're the man, Jools. Let me talk to the rest of the band. Give me your number. I'll get back to you."

Then, with a false grin, Lance was gone.

Jools stood alone, his mind in a state of shock. He knew most kids saw him as a nerd. Now, he was all set to join the best band in school.

Chapter 2 - Stab in the Back

Lance sat in the school dining room with Jade and Suzie, the singers in his band, Elite. The two girls laughed a lot and talked in loud voices, but their eyes were cold. Lance didn't see this. He was too busy thinking how funny his jokes were.

His mobile beeped. It was a text from Zak:

```
TELL THE REST, FORGET IT.
WE' LL WIN. NO PROBS.
```

Lance showed the message to the girls. They grinned.

"Hey, we've got a new keyboard player," said Lance.

"Who?" asked Jade.

"Jools."

"The fat guy?" asked Suzie, her eyes open wide.

"Well, that's what I told him today and he thinks it's true. Is he a loser or what?"

"Let's text him," said Jade, with a mean smile.

"Yeah, do it," said Suzie.

Lance got busy with his mobile. At the table behind them, a tall girl stood up. She had heard every word and her face was dark with rage.

She left the room without a word.

Chapter 3 - The 'Losers'

Jools sat alone on a bench in the school yard.

He had a mobile, but it hardly ever rang. He didn't have many friends. So when he heard the bleep of a text he was happy, until he read it:

```
YOU IN ELITE?
NO WAY LOSER.
```

"They're pathetic."

Jools looked up. A tall girl with wild red hair and big bright eyes was staring at him.

"I heard what they said about you."

"Right," said Jools. His voice was quiet.

"Look, my name's Cass and I know how you feel. I get a hard time from other kids all the time. I guess I look a bit wild, so they call me 'Crazy'. And do I care? No way."

Jools liked Cass. She was strong and she made him smile

"Do you really play keyboards?"
Cass asked.

"Yes."

"Any good?"

"Not bad."

"That's it then," said Cass.

"What?" Jools asked.

"You play. I sing. We'll form our own band for Dream Stars."

"Okay," grinned Jools. "What shall we call it?"

"How about 'The Losers'?"

Cass laughed so loud, kids in the school yard turned to stare. She didn't see them. Her mind was buzzing. She knew who she wanted in the new band and she was sure they would go for it.

Cass rushed off to find them. There was no time to lose.

Chapter 4 - We are Nervous

The next day was Saturday. Jools sat at home writing a dance track. He didn't look like a pop star, but his music was great.

He sat back in his chair. He needed a break, so he checked his email. He had one new message.

Jools

From: Cass

To: Jools

Date: 1 November

Subject: The Losers

Hi Jools

Two more losers now in the band. Meet at my place noon today. 16 Beech Road. Bring all your music stuff. Let's go for it.

Cass

The mood in the garage at Cass's house was edgy.

"It's a stupid name," said Jay, the band's new drummer. He was small and wiry and never sat still.

"Very uncool," said Mina, from behind her dark sunglasses. To Mina, things were either cool or uncool.

Jay and Mina were in the year below Cass and Jools at school. Cass had saved them both from bullies in the past. Now she wanted to see them shine.

"They call us all losers at school. That's why the name's perfect," said Cass. "Can't you see? The joke's on them."

"They won't see that," said Jools.

"They'll just laugh at us."

"You think of a name then," snapped
Cass.

They all sat in silence, thinking of the
Dream Stars show that was just two
weeks away.

"Looking at you lot now, I think we should call ourselves Nervous!"
said Jay.

Cass's mad laugh shook the garage. The others joined in. The band had a name.

* * * *

They spent the rest of the day making music. Jools played them his new dance track.

When he hit the keyboards, the band came alive.

Cass started rapping.

I'm shaking like a kitten,
Jumpy as a frog.
I cry like a baby,
Howl like a dog.

I'm Nervous.
N-n-n-Nervous.
Nervous as I can be!

The band played their new song over and over again and every time it got better.

"Losers?" said Jay with a grin. "No way!"

Chapter 5 - Dirty Tricks

A couple of weeks later, the big day arrived. The Dream Stars show was due to start at seven in the school hall. That afternoon there was a full rehearsal. Every band and singer had to do one song.

Elite were sure they would win, until they heard Nervous play. Then their smiles faded. Lance walked across to Dan Butcher, the school's hardest bully, who was watching the bands with a scowl on his face.

"What?" growled Dan.

"Money," said Lance. "Want to make some?"

Cass saw Lance and Dan staring at her. She didn't know what they were saying, but she knew it was bad news...

Chapter 6 -
So Near Yet So Far

By seven, the school hall was full and Nervous were on stage. Jools felt his hands start to shake. This was like a bad dream. Jay hit the drums. Mina's bass guitar came in next. She sounded good.

Then Jools tried to play, but his keyboards were dead. Someone had switched off the power. Cass tried to sing, but her mike was off too. Panic set in. Jay and Mina stopped playing. Jools ran off to plug the power back in.

At the back of the hall, Dan Butcher's gang started to chant and stamp their feet:

"Nerds! Nerds! Nerds!"

At the side of the stage, Lance smiled.

"That's fixed them," he told Zak.

For once, Cass was lost for words. Mina's sunglasses hid the tears of anger that were burning in her eyes. Then Jay started to play his drums again. He hit them very hard, in time with the hard kids chanting at the back.

Cass heard her mike whistle. The power was back on. She grabbed the mike and started a chant of her own. Her eyes were flashing now and a big grin lit her face.

"Nerds... rule! Nerds... rule!"

Jools ran back on stage and his keyboards burst into life. Nervous sounded great.

All the kids in the hall were laughing at the bullies now. Cass had made them look small. Lance watched Butcher rush out of the room. His face was sour and angry.

Up on the stage, Cass was having the time of her life.

"We'd like to do a song for you now," she yelled. "We wrote it and we hope you like it. It's called 'N-n-n-Nervous'."

The song they wrote in the garage went down a storm. Nervous left the stage to huge cheers. They were a hit.

But Elite were even better. They had a backing track of bass and drums to fill out the sound of their guitars and their lead singers, Jade and Suzie, looked and sang like real pop stars.

Nervous got second prize. They knew the best band had won. "So near, yet so far," said Cass to Jools, as they received their CD tokens from the judges.

Jools didn't reply. He ran off into the wings of the stage. Cass was shocked. She didn't think he would be such a bad loser.

Chapter 7 - Final Twist

"The next time you hear this song will be on Chart Zone FM," said Mr Simpson, the teacher who had run the Dream Stars contest. "Here with 'I Know I'm The Best', it's Elite!"

The crowd cheered. Then there was silence. Elite looked nervous. A teacher ran onstage.

"Elite's backing track has gone missing," said Mr Simpson, through the mike. "But I'm sure that won't worry them. Let's hear it again for Elite!"

Without the bass and drums on their backing track, Elite's music was weak.

Lance and Zak turned their electric guitars up loud and did the best they could. Things were okay until Jade and Suzie started to sing. They sounded like two stray cats howling at the moon.

One by one, the kids in the hall saw the truth. Jade and Suzie couldn't sing. They had mimed to the voices of other singers on the backing track. Elite were cheats. Soon the music was drowned out by the jeers of the crowd. There was no place to hide.

Elite ran off the stage in shame.

Cass saw Jools at the side of the stage. He gave her a sly smile, then pulled a CD out of his jacket pocket. Cass knew what was on it. Elite's backing track!

Chapter 8 - Radio Stars

Nervous were sitting in Cass's garage eating pizza.

Time had raced past in a wild rush. They had been to Red Fox Studios and made their CD of 'N-n-n-Nervous'. Now it was going to be played on Chart Zone FM.

"I could see they were miming," Jools was saying. "I hate cheats."

"Shush," said Cass. "This is it!"

She turned the radio up loud.

"And now the new single from a young band who won the Dream Stars talent show at Highmoor School a couple of weeks back. This is 'N-n-n-Nervous'!"

Mina jumped to her feet and started dancing.

In seconds, the rest of them were singing and dancing too.

"We'll have to change our name," shouted Cass.

"Why?" asked Jay.

"We're not Nervous now, are we?"

"Nerds rule," chanted Jools.

"Right," said Mina. "Cool."